YES, MRS. SMITH

More Money than Time

Book 1

T. Scott

Published by: I.S.I. Publishing LLC, P.O. Box 29037, Parma, Ohio 44129

Email: info@isipublishingllc.com
Website: www.isipublishingllc.com

ISBN (Paperback): 979-8-9920157-8-2
ISBN (eBook): 979-8-9920157-9-9

Edited by: Anthony W. Scott, Esq. / I.S.I. Publishing

First Edition

Printed in the United States of America.

For bulk order discounts or special inquiries, please contact info@isipublishingllc.com

Acknowledgments

Thank you to everyone who encouraged me to write from a place of fun and authenticity. Writing my non-fiction books was as much a part of me as this book. I labored over whether I could fully be myself or whether I needed to hide behind a pseudonym.

More books will come from Anthony W. Scott, Esq. For now, however, it's T. Scott's season.

Special thanks to my Beta Readers, my old and new friends. Within the next two days, this book will be in your hands. You will be the first to help unleash this part of me in writing…a side that some have never met or haven't seen in decades.

Last but never least, thank you to my Helpmate, my Muse, my Wife.

I dedicate this work to you, my Milagro.

Note from the Author

This book centers on a single moment and the intimacy of an erotic encounter. It is intentionally plot-light and not intended to explore full character development. Consider this a snapshot rather than a journey.

Trigger Warning & Reader Advisory

Before you dive into this branch of this Universe, there are a few things you should know. This story contains themes and scenes that may trigger or be uncomfortable for some readers, including:

Explicit sensual content (adults behaving like adults… very enthusiastic and explorative adults).

Consensual sexual fluid play and explicit descriptions of bodily sexual responses.

Power imbalances woven into consensual relationships.

Age-gap interactions.

Manipulation, seduction, and blurred moral lines.

Financial dominance / gift-giving dynamics.

Infidelity, secrets, and emotionally charged entanglements.

Mature language and scenarios that are not suitable for younger audiences.

Physical discipline, impact choking, and breath play between consenting adults.

This book is intended for 18+ readers who enjoy a mix of:

Powerful and Mature Women.

Luxury fantasy.

Complicated emotions.

Ethically gray areas.

Smart characters making questionable choices.

If any of the above feels like too much… it is okay to set the book down.

If it feels like exactly what you came for… please turn the page.

Contents

Prologue

"Of course, I will be ready, Mrs. Clay. If I ever disappointed you, you would not have booked my flight or scheduled my fee."

She knew Aaron was teasing, but he was not wrong. Over the last couple of years, he had been worth every dollar she had paid for his "attention". Without question, he was the best referral she had ever received.

"Alright, alright," she paused. "Professor Simon."

Aaron chuckled.

"My driver will be at Gate 13. We'll go straight to our reservations. Please wear the dark gray suit I sent."

"Don't worry. I know what is required. I need to finish my morning routine now."

"Understood, sir. I get impatient between your visits." Her pout was clear, even through the phone.

"Mrs. Clay."

His voice had become stern. Erica (Mrs. Clay, when he was not pleased with her) knew her brattiness was not being indulged this morning.

"See you tomorrow. Be ready. Stretch and drink Gatorade—you do not want a repeat of last time."

The last time they were together, she cramped fiercely… just as she was about to cum. She lost her balance, and, given how their legs were intertwined, they fell to the floor. Hard!

"Yes, Professor Simon, I can't stand you. See you tomorrow, and travel safely. Bye, sir."

The attempt to lighten the mood failed; Aaron had already hung up.

The phone call ended, leaving Erica anticipating the weekend ahead. Meanwhile, Aaron prepared to tackle his day.

His weekdays always started at 4:00 am with a workout, sauna, coffee, and fruit before a 7:00 a.m. start. As usual, the sauna was empty when he stepped inside. He muted his watch, letting the heat envelop him. With two hours before his first meeting, he let his mind drift over how charmed his life had become.

Meet Aaron Simon

Aaron Simon has accomplished a lot in his 34 years. He serves as an adjunct professor at the Ellison School of International Business at New York University and as one of the youngest vice presidents in the Global Markets & International Strategy Division at Fulcrum, Snyder & McCloskey's global headquarters.

He is successful, articulate, and rarely without a warm smile or a kind word for others. Although affluent, he lives modestly. He was raised in the church and taught to be humble, polite, and respectful.

People find Aaron charming and handsome. He has been described as a combination of a younger Idris Elba and Michael B. Jordan. His wardrobe was immaculately maintained. Although once a scrawny teen, he now stands 6′1″ - 6′2″ on a good day. He kept his muscular frame at a consistent 210-212 lbs. Unlike most people he knew, he had no tattoos or piercings. Aaron's surprisingly deep baritone contrasted with his youthful appearance. Except for an occasional cigar or cocktail, he strictly adhered to his eating, sleeping, and exercise regimen.

People who did not know Aaron's background would have thought he came from the best of everything: private schools, gated communities, and summers abroad.

They certainly would never fathom that he was an internationally sought-after escort.

The Auction

During his senior year of college, Aaron saw an advertisement for a bachelor auction and, if selected, would be paid $1,000, plus any expenses he incurred on the date. That $1,000 was built into the bidder's pledge, with all bids starting at $2,000.

The auction was held at a lavish club called The Vault. All the proceeds went to help victims of sexual abuse and trafficking.

From the outside, the club did not look like anything special. The interior was quite different. This could not have been the same building. The transformation was magical. As soon as you entered the club, it was as if you were in an opulent museum. The ceilings were vaulted as if within a chapel. Marble columns and bar tops adorned the room where the auction was being held. An endless number of candles illuminated and gently heated countless corridors.

Aaron had never been much of a clubber or a drinker, but the matching bars seemed to have every drink ever known to man. The top shelf could be reached only with mobile ladders comparable to those in the world's largest bookstores.

He could hear what sounded like water from another side of one of the columns.

What the hell…

He stopped in his tracks and looked up. There was a waterfall situated next to one of the bars. He abruptly turned, as the sound he had been hearing was not just the waterfall. There was a fountain in the middle of one of the adjoining rooms.

A frickin' fountain in the middle of a club. This is NOT Kansas anymore, Toto.

He shook his head in disbelief and went to find a seat. This was unlike anything he had ever set his eyes on.

Aaron was not the first person to arrive. He saw some of Atlanta's "who's who" being auctioned off. Business people he admired, athletes, and actors were all on display. He was intimidated by being in this mix of people. He kicked himself for wasting the networking opportunity as he sheepishly just sat in the corner, waiting for things to commence.

The lineup was revealed. A total of eighteen people were going to be auctioned off. His number was ten. He was not the first nor the last, which made him feel a bit more confident. That did not last long. The host, Ursula, would call people up one by one, read a bit of their bios, and then the person—male or female—would do "their thang."

Some would sing, tell jokes, or offer a monologue. One person even ripped off his clothes and started flexing his muscular frame.

Aaron was nauseous.

What have I gotten myself into?

It was weird. Women were bidding on women as well as men bidding on men. There were even two twin brothers with tattoos prominently visible from under their suits. They were bidding on everyone who came to the stage.

This shit is so weird. This is a weird-ass charity.

Some people were going for just the $2,000 low bid. Others had gone as high as $50,000. He feared he would be the lowest bidder of the night.

Ugh…that would be so damn embarrassing.

He felt so out of place and was thinking of sneaking out before he was called. He was so focused on an escape plan that he didn't notice a beautiful server standing over him.

Misty

Aaron's mouth hung wide open when he realized she was there. She was gorgeous. He could tell she was older than him, but not by much. She was extremely light-complexioned, but he could tell she was black. Or, she had to, at least, be mixed. He had never seen blue eyes like hers on a Black person.

She leaned over and placed a shot of something auburn and steaming on the table next to his sweaty palms.

"Here you go, sugah." Her Cajun drawl sounded as if she were from New Orleans.

"Ummm… I did not order anything, Ms…"

"Misty. I am just Misty," she clarified as she pointed to the name tag above her subtle and perky breasts.

"Misty, sorry… I did not order anything, Ms. Misty."

"I know, baby. You could not afford anything here anyway." She winked affectionately at him as she made a joke at his expense. "It's a gift from an admirer."

She could see his hesitancy as he stared at the drink.

"What is it?"

Leaning in, she came intimately close to his lips.

"That, my love, is a secret."

He could smell her fragrance. It reminded him of a sunny day at the beach.

"But I tell you what, sugah, I'll have one with you so that you know it is not poison."

He was so transfixed looking into her eyes that he did not notice that she had raised a second shot of the reddish-brown liquor to her lips. With her free hand, she nudged his shot towards him.

"Cheers, handsome." She raised her glass and held it. The piercing stare became insistent as her eyes went to the shot, and back to his. The flirtation had subsided. This was a command.

He picked up the shot glass hesitantly and raised it. Her intensity returned to flirtation. She wrapped her arm around his arm affectionately, intertwining them like lovers. Their eyes locked as they both took the shot.

Aaron began to cough, minimally at first, but it quickly became violent.

Misty raised two fingers to Aaron's lips. The violent cough subsided unnaturally quickly.

She opened the rest of her hand to grip Aaron's chin, subtly tickling his goatee. She pulled his face to hers and gave a subtle kiss. It was a simple, quaint, but intimate touch of her violet-shaded lips to his.

"Knock 'em dead, sugah," she said as she wiped her lipstick off his lips.

Coming Next to the Stage

"Next, I would like to introduce our next bachelor, Mr. Aaron Simmons."

His name being called distracted Aaron. He looked toward the stage, realizing he had no chance of escaping at this point. He turned around to look for Misty as he stood up, yet did not see her.

Hesitantly, Aaron walked to the stage.

Fuck, where did all these people come from?

"Come on, Aaron. Let us see you, love."

Aaron approached the stage, "Actually... it is Simon, not Simmons."

Ursula looked at Aaron knowingly and smiled.

"Why, yes, it is, love. Thank you so much for correcting me." Returning the microphone to her face, she resumed the introduction.

"Beloved Guests, please welcome our next candidate this afternoon, Mr. Aaron Simon. Mr. Simon is a promising young man with a bright future. He has a stellar grade point average. 4.15, I believe. He is brilliant. Great for breeding..."

Aaron looked at Ursula sharply, "Huh...?"

Ursula chuckled, and all the crowd broke into laughter, except for Aaron.

"In all seriousness, Aaron's goals are to complete his undergraduate degree, obtain his master's degree, and make lots of money so he can help people. He volunteered for our auction this afternoon so that he can help raise money for charity; specifically, he wants to help prevent human trafficking."

She paused, looked at Aaron in an unsettling way, and subtly licked the corners of her lips.

"And finally, from what I can see, this exquisite gentleman has a big dick. Trust me, I know these things. He will work overtime to please you. And you know that the beauty of young men is that they have stamina that can keep going into overtime, as many of you demand. Isn't that right, Master Aaron?"

She grabbed Aaron's dick and squeezed it tightly, her nails slightly digging into him. Aaron was entirely taken by surprise. By the time he opened his mouth to protest, Ursula had released his dick, raised her hand, and called for the first bid of $2,000.

The bids escalated slowly. Everyone was bidding to get their hands on his obedient young flesh. At first.

Aaron was stunned. He had to do something; he just had no clue what. Slowly and awkwardly, his body began to gyrate—a feeble attempt at a striptease. The bids were starting to wane. So was the crowd's interest.

Why did I sign up for this?

Then... a collective hush came across the room. Nobody, not even Aaron, moved for what felt like a painfully long instant. Then he heard heels clicking slowly. Loudly. Echoing. The crowd parted for her. She stared at him. He could not look away. He saw only her. He felt her before he saw her.

She had to be at least fifteen years older than Aaron. At least that was what he presumed. But she was fucking gorgeous. Not that he had much experience, but he had always been a fan of mature women. Boys his age were fantasizing about girls like Rihanna, Beyoncé, and Nikki Minaj. But women like Sanaa Lathan, Regina King, and Nia Long filled his deepest fantasies.

Her gray hair was cut in a short pixie style. Tight curls adorned the top of her head. Hints of formerly jet-black hair were intertwined with the gray and white strands. Longer curls effortlessly hung over her left eye. She continued to push it back from her face so she could see Aaron more clearly, devouring his frame with her eyes.

Her body was phenomenal. She was as shapely as Angela Bassett in *What's Love Got to Do It*. Her shoulders and arms were equally as sculpted as Angela looked in the movie. Those spaghetti straps hung effortlessly on her shoulders. He tried to regain his composure. He could not.

An electric guitar broke the chilling silence, "Mmm-wahhh… dumm… dumm… mmm-wahhh…." It sounded familiar. It paused and echoed "Mmm-wahhh… dumm… dumm… mmm-wahhh…."

Aaron knew that song. It was "Untitled (How Does it Feel)" by D'Angelo.

Nobody in the room was as surprised as he was when he started lip-syncing the words. Eyes locked on this mystery woman.

Girl, it's only you. Have it your way...

Their eyes remained glued. He opened the first button of his shirt. Second button.

I can provide everything that you desire...

Third button. The shirt was now lying on the ground. His surprisingly chiseled chest, shoulders, and arms were exposed.

His belt was tossed next to the shirt.

The gyrations were vastly improved from earlier. This looked like a completely new man. Pants' buttons unbuttoned. Pants Unzipped.

Aaron had no clue what he was doing, nor how far he was going. He felt that he was still at the back of the room after finishing that shot. He was watching himself because this could not be him.

How does it feel? Yeah

How does it feel? Yeah, yeah

Pants on the floor. Stepping out of them. Through his underwear, the room could now see it… Nine or ten inches of dick, blessed with girth. And it was staring at her and only her.

Aaron was innately shy. However, he learned how to put on a good show from the church choir, various school plays, and speech and debate competitions. Nonetheless, even he realized how different his performance was from his normal personality. Something had moved him, and he liked it.

The crowd was in a frenzy as he sexily danced for them while lip-syncing. The sounds of frenzied bidders drowned out the song.

Are People actually bidding on me?

The woman raised her hand for the first and only time that night. That same hush enveloped the room again. He was speechless when he heard the final amount—$20,000.

She had bought him for the night.

Or, for however long she wanted him.

Yes, Mrs. Smith

The woman who won him was a majestic-looking, older Black woman. After having put his clothes back on, he sought her out in a more secluded lounge area of the club. He wandered about in awe of all the celebrities he noticed.

"Good evening, Aaron." Her soft and sultry voice snapped him out of his trance. He wondered how she knew his name. She must have noticed the perplexed look on his face.

"Your name and bio were in the program." He literally had forgotten. For such an intellectual man, he had become instantly stupid.

"That was quite a performance you put on, young man. Was it for me?"

"Thank you. I am glad that you liked it. Honestly, I surprised myself, Ms…"

"I am Mrs. Lydia Smith. You may call me Mrs. Smith until I say otherwise."

"Yes, Ms. Smith."

"No. I said, 'Mrs.' I am a married woman."

She raised her left hand, and Aaron saw the largest diamond he had ever seen. It rested comfortably on her immaculately manicured hand.

"It is my pleasure to meet you, Mrs. Smith," Aaron awkwardly stammered.

Her hand was still raised, as if waiting for Aaron to kiss it. He had seen that in movies but had never done it in person. Nervously, he reached for her hand to kiss it. His lips were gentle on her hand. He looked up and saw her approving glance.

"Good boy," she purred.

"Thank you, ma'am," he said in a quizzical voice.

Her eyes cut sharply. "I instructed you to call me Mrs. Smith," she said, her voice chilling. "I was under the impression you were intelligent and articulate, Mr. Simon."

Heat crawled up his neck. "Yes, Mrs. Smith," he corrected, the words catching in his throat.

Aaron was surprisingly intimidated by how forceful she had become. "I am Ma… I mean, I am intelligent, Mrs. Smith."

No woman had ever spoken to him like that before. He felt himself growing, uncomfortably scraping against his zipper. He fought the urge to adjust himself.

She softly bit the right corner of her bottom lip. She enjoyed his immediate obedience and his visible discomfort.

"Aaron, I presume that you have never participated in a charity auction before, correct?"

"No, Mrs. Smith, I have not. I thought it would be great to support a worthy cause and to meet wonderful people like you. I am a student…."

"Yes. Yes, I know," she interrupted. She was becoming exasperated with Aaron.

Mrs. Smith continued, "You attend Georgia Tech. and have remarkable grades in your finance program. You hail from a small town in Ohio. I read all of that in your bio, Aaron."

He realized from her tone that he was frustrating her. He felt as if he were being chastised. He wanted to say something, but he did not know what. Plus, he needed that $1,000.

He wondered whether she could cancel her donation if he said something she found stupid or disrespectful. Nothing in his mind suggested she would accept anything remotely construed as rude. He wanted to change the subject.

"Yes, of course, you did say that. I'm sorry."

She sighed. "Aaron, you never say 'I am sorry' for anything. I already know you are a brilliant and beautiful Black man. What I can see quickly is that you have more charisma and charm than you realize… yet."

"If you are wrong, incorrect, or misspoke, the most deferential thing you should say is, 'I apologize.' Do you understand that? Do you understand the difference?"

Confusingly, his dick had started to bulge in his pants.

Her eyes glanced at the growing sight. It held her glare longer than she expected. His slacks couldn't hide the growth cascading towards her thigh.

She was gorgeous, sure. But he had never been spoken to like that before. He needed to redirect the conversation.

"Yes, I do understand," oblivious to her distraction.

"Excellent. We will get along swimmingly." Finally, Mrs. Smith averted her glare from his imprint. Softly, she stroked his facial stubble with the back of her hand.

He soaked up her touch, starved for her approval. He knew what support and praise felt like. He had not lacked attention or encouragement as a child.

This was different. She was teaching him, pouring into him even as she berated him. It was confusing yet intoxicating.

Mrs. Smith softly cleared her throat to bring him back from wherever his thoughts had strayed.

"Um… what would you like to do for the rest of our time together, Mrs. Smith?" Aaron asked with feigned confidence. "They shared a lot of different places we can go to once the auction is over."

She quietly looked at Aaron for a few moments. Yet to him, it felt like minutes had passed. He felt out of his league in the conversation and hated it. He stood there quietly.

She gave him a knowing smile and walked slowly toward him. She left little space between them as she looked into his eyes. Even with heels on, she was still shorter than Aaron. At best, she was 5'6"-5'8" with heels. Nonetheless, he felt as if he were looking up at her. She seemed powerful to him.

Eventually, Mrs. Smith broke the silence and eased Aaron's discomfort.

"Aaron, my dear… dear beautiful man. I just spent $20,000 on you. I have no intention of going to some museum, gathering, or whatever little event that they cooked up. Do you understand me?"

"Yes, Ma-," he proudly caught himself. "Yes, I understand, Mrs. Smith."

"Good. So, what is going to happen is you are going to go. You are going to the bar and bringing back an Amaretto Sour for me. I want to learn more about you… the things not in your bio."

"Yes, Mrs. Smith." As he turned to walk away, she added, "While you are there, get yourself a drink, too."

"Thank you, I shouldn't. I don't really drink, and the bartender already gave me one earlier."

"You do now," she commanded. "You will have a strong yet refined cocktail—something befitting a man of your potential. Order a single pour, neat, of Angel's Envy. Tell them to pour your cocktail into a Glencairn glass and mine into a rocks glass. I want an ice sphere in mine. Did you get all that?"

"Yes, I believe I did."

"Very well," she said as she gestured for him to proceed.

He quickly came to appreciate her praise. His confidence was growing. Only now did he realize he lacked it.

Time to Go

They sat there for hours, just talking and having a few more cocktails. After he painfully choked down the Angel's Envy, she suggested he try an Old Fashioned. The sweet combination of vanilla, citrus, and whiskey became the night's go-to drink.

It loosened Aaron up and stripped away his nervousness. He shared that he had come from the Midwest, from a poor community called East Cleveland, Ohio. A "STEM" kid growing up, he loved studying science, technology, engineering, and mathematics. As a child, he knew he did not want to be a police officer, a football player, or a lawyer. He wanted to work in finance and have an essential job on Wall Street.

She was also loosening up. She found him genuinely fascinating, far more than just the pretty face she had bid on a few hours earlier. The scolding and chastisement had subsided. She shared stories of her travels and experiences in foreign lands. Aside from Georgia, he had not traveled anywhere else, but he knew he wanted to.

He could not believe all the experiences she had had. She was unlike anyone he had ever met.

The event had ended, and the club was opening to its regular clientele. Lydia knew The Vault was an exclusive lifestyle club because she was a longtime member. However, she had no intention of exposing Aaron to it. At least, not yet.

"So, Aaron…" Mrs. Smith whispered. "I have enjoyed my time with you. You are such an impressive specimen of a man." It is getting late, and we should be leaving. This place starts to look quite different at this time of evening.

"I have also, Mrs. Smith," Aaron echoed. His demeanor had returned to its usual confidence.

"Your life has been so impressive; you have done so many things. Do you think we can keep in touch?"

She laughed loudly at Aaron. "You are so cute, Aaron. Let me be clear. We are leaving here together. Our night is nowhere near over."

Her tone shifted. She stood and walked in front of Aaron. Her thighs were now touching him.

"To be clear, I paid $20,000 for you. I can do whatever I want with you."

"You are a scrumptious young chocolate man, exactly what I like. Pretty. Smart. I am just as confident you have a big dick, an eager tongue, and strong second and third rounds."

"But I see more."

She squeezed his dick as she said it. It was as rigid as steel. She had noticed his restraint all night. It impressed her. It came to life in her hands. She wanted to see it. To feel it. To taste it. To explode on it.

Her breasts were directly in front of his face. He had noticed them several times during the evening, but this was the first time he realized she wasn't wearing a bra. Nipples screamed to be released.

She stepped away from him. She was wet and tired of talking, at least here. She reached into her clutch and grabbed her car keys.

"Aaron, you are driving me home tonight," she commanded as she handed him the keys to her Mercedes. "I sent my driver home hours ago."

Aaron stood up. His engorged dick pressed painfully against his pants. He tried to adjust as he reached for the keys, subtly.

"Yes, ma'am."

She smacked him so hard that his head turned. He snapped his head back. His mind raced. Nothing about this seemed negotiable.

He wanted to leave, but his legs betrayed him. He couldn't move.

What the hell.

"I have instructed you on multiple occasions about how you will address me. You will learn to follow orders."

"Do not get me wrong," she continued, this time with her hand in his face. "I like you, Aaron, I sincerely do. And I am going to enjoy fucking you tonight and in the morning. I genuinely believe it will be good. I hope you do not disappoint me."

"Obedience and trust are crucial to me. Getting you to obey will not be difficult. I know this, even though you are slightly slower than I expected."

"Do you want to be obedient, Mr. Simon?"

Did she call me "Mr."?

Sheepishly, Aaron responded, "Yes, Mrs. Smith. Yes, I do."

"That is wonderful. I do not enjoy disciplining my students. Would you like to be my student, Aaron?"

"Yes, Mrs. Smith."

"That is obedience… But trust… your trust must be freely given. Would you like to give me your trust, Aaron?"

To his own surprise, he did not hesitate. Enthusiasm outweighed sound judgment. "Yes, Mrs. Smith. I would like that."

Remembering his manners, he said, "I would like that very much, please."

"Very good. If you please me as I require, I will keep you. You will belong to me. You will be very well taken care of… and that will be quite beneficial for you and me. Would you like that?"

Tongue-tied, Aaron nodded.

What just happened?

"… But first, you will learn to follow basic commands. You will become a confident and strong man. Until then…"

Her voice trailed off as she slammed her hand into his face. It was like Halle Berry smacking Eddie Murphy in Boomerang. Aaron fell back into his seat.

She grabbed his hand and pulled it inside the split of her dress. He instantly forgot how to speak or think. He forgot she had just slapped the shit out of him and mashed him. All he felt was her warmth as she guided two fingers inside her.

No sooner had he felt the wetness on his fingers than she pulled his hand back out of her.

"Now place your fingers in your mouth."

Aaron obediently and silently complied. He could not believe this was what came from responding to an ad. His eyes closed as he placed his two fingers in his mouth. They were thick with her wetness, not in a negative way by far. She smelled so damn good.

I cannot believe this is happening.

He could feel her juices on his fingers. She stood so close that he could now smell them coming directly from her body. They tasted fresh. Aaron detected a faint pineapple flavor in her juices. He continued to lick his fingers, in part because they tasted wonderful, and in part because he did not want to upset her again.

"Aaron! Stop sucking my juice out through your fingers and get the car, please and thank you." Her tone was softer, sultrier. It had returned to the voice she had first used when she spoke to him.

"Yes, Mrs. Smith."

Aaron turned quickly to run to the car. Before he could step off, however, she grabbed his arm. She flung him around and kissed him passionately. Aaron was taken off guard. At one point, his teeth scraped against hers. She grabbed his pants, squeezing his dick. He breathed in deeply. Her forceful grip felt just right.

He exhaled, and their tongues intertwined. They were in unison for a moment. Their bodies were pressed together.

She pulled back from him and looked him in the eye. He stood there, staring back. He did not notice her hand moving toward his face until it was beside him. He flinched, expecting to be smacked again.

"I apologize, Aaron." It sounded sincere. She then placed her two fingers in his mouth, and they tasted and smelled the same as his hand. She had been touching herself and him as they shared their first, but far from last, kiss.

"I am ready for you to take me home now, Aaron."

Do You Trust Me?

Aaron was slightly buzzed and should not have been driving. The fall night air shook him out of his slight trance. He was back in his own head.

What am I doing? This is crazy. Wait. Why am I...?

His inner thoughts screeched to a halt when he heard her moan. Mrs. Smith had pulled up her dress. Her pussy was shaved bald except for a small landing strip of hair. It matched the same beautiful shade of gray atop her head. She was now touching herself aggressively. She was violently thrusting two middle fingers in and out of herself. She would periodically slow down or stop altogether, squeezing her legs together to increase the intensity.

During one of those pauses, she pulled down one of the straps on her dress. Aaron focused on her perfectly shaped breasts. With one hand, she continued to masturbate while the other aggressively massaged her breasts. Occasionally, she stopped to pull and twist her nipples. Aaron felt himself staring at her, oblivious to the road. Drool dripped onto his slacks.

"Left turn," OnStar chimed in.

He began to turn without even looking at the road.

"BLLLAAAATTTTT" blared from the Ford F-150's horn. "Watch where the fuck you are going, kid!" Aaron jerked the wheel to the right, trying to avoid the oncoming truck. He overcompensated, and the car almost jumped the curb.

"Sorry."

Aaron looked back at Mrs. Smith. The near-fatal car crash had not stopped her at all. If anything, it had turned her on even more. She had shifted her body, leaning more toward the driver's seat. She was staring at Aaron as she fucked herself with three fingers. She fought the urge to close her eyes. She wanted to see how engrossed Aaron was in this performance. His dick was bursting through his pants.

She still masturbated for the rest of the drive. Not once did she allow herself to have an orgasm. She just kept building the intensity.

Eventually, Aaron got them safely to her townhome in the Tuxedo Park community. It was tucked away in a gated community. Like most of these affluent neighborhoods, the houses seemed stacked on top of one another. Each could peer into the others' homes, if not for high gates and ornate fences.

But not the Smiths. Their home sat near the end of the road, isolated. There was enough space on both sides of their home to fit another mini mansion, but nothing was there. It was their own corner of the world, cut off from anyone not invited.

The yard was immaculate, as if the landscapers had just left a moment ago.

Aaron pulled the car into the three-car garage. He never noticed her move, yet the door opened as if it were waiting.

"You have reached your destination. Welcome home, Mrs. Smith."

Mrs. Smith had hopped out of the car before it had even come to a complete stop.

"Let yourself in and make yourself comfortable."

The garage was connected to the kitchen. Aaron took off his shoes before coming in, as he had been raised. He walked through the kitchen toward what looked like the living room. The interior of the house was even more impressive than the exterior. High, vaulted ceilings in the living room made the house feel larger than it was. The house was dimly lit. An abundance of candles provided the only light in the living room. The scent of lavender filled the room. John Coltrane played softly throughout the house.

Countless pieces of artwork adorned every wall. Nothing was to his taste, nor did it look familiar, yet he presumed they were expensive. Despite the warmth of the fireplace, the room felt cold. It looked like a museum. It was as if no one lived here. In the far corner of the living room, beneath the winding staircase, sat an elegant Steinway piano. Aaron admired the piano's beauty, fearful of touching it.

"Do you play?'

Aaron was startled by a man's deep voice. He was so distracted that he had not noticed a large, muscular, older Black man standing in a doorway, just watching him. This guy looked like he could really do damage if he hit someone.

"I'm sorry if I startled you, young man."

The large male approached Aaron. Aaron's body tensed up as the man extended his hand.

"Smith, Devlin Smith… and you are?"

"My name is Aaron, sir, Aaron Simon."

"Pleasure to meet you, Aaron Simon. Are you here to fuck my wife?"

Shit, here it comes. This is all bad.

"So-so-sorry, sir," Aaron stuttered. His voice made it clear he was seeking clarity.

"I said, 'Are you here to fuck my wife?'"

With perfect timing, Mrs. Smith walked into the room.

"Hello, my love. I see you have met my new friend, Aaron." She greeted Mr. Smith with a kiss on the lips. It was not enthusiastic; it was just routine.

"I did not know you had already made it back home. I was not expecting you for another day or so. I would have invited you to the auction. As you can see, they had some nice options this time."

Devlin looked at Aaron briefly and cracked a subtle, approving smile.

"No worries, dear. I had other plans once I returned."

"Ohhh, is your friend here, Dev?"

"Yes, love, he is…"

There was slight tension in their comments, but it was nowhere near as tense as you would expect from a couple where both had lovers in the household at the same time.

Mr. and Mrs. Smith had an arrangement that let them satisfy their appetites elsewhere. They just had to remain discreet. That was the rule. Sometimes they visited the Vault and other such establishments together, but they often separated once they arrived.

"Oh, well, in that case, please do not keep me waiting," she said, a hint of pettiness in her voice.

"No worries at all, hun."

"Dev, can you undress me, please, dear?"

"Of course."

Aaron shyly looked down.

"Aaron," Mrs. Smith commanded. "Do not look away!"

Dev waited for the exchange to finish. He chuckled to himself, knowing his wife's admonishments all too well. He knew none of them could look away; all their eyes must remain locked in this seduction.

Seductively, Devlin wrapped his arms around her waist. Slowly, he followed every curve of her body. He may have been fluid with his sexuality, but he has always enjoyed Lydia's body. His wife of 30 years is still exquisite to him. He could see in Aaron's young eyes that he felt the same way. As he brushed his hands across her breasts and to the straps of her dress, his eyes never left Aaron. He saw the conflict in the young man's face. Devlin was enjoying this game far too much as he let the dress drop to the floor.

Dammmnnn. She was perfect. The most beautiful woman I had ever seen.

Despite unquestionably being turned on, Aaron's nerves had taken over.

Devlin and Lydia both found his visible discomfort amusing. He returned to tracing his wife's curves slowly. Softly, he left kisses all over her body as he bent over to pick up the dress. All eyes were still locked on each other.

Mrs. Smith extended her hand towards Aaron. He did not move. He just stood there looking at them both. They looked back at him. Her arm remained extended. Disapprovingly, she extended her arm again, making it clear that this was not a request. It was a directive.

Aaron took her hand to assist her as she stepped out of the dress on the floor. Her elegantly painted toes were now showing as she stepped out of her heels.

Eyes were still locked on Aaron, "Dev… I have an amazing idea. Would you and your friend like to join us?"

Aaron's jaw dropped. "Um, Mrs. Smith…. I…"

"Don't worry, Aaron, I was just kidding. I would not do that to you…yet."

She winked at Devlin, causing him to smile. They both realized that they had gone too far with that last comment.

"No worries, Aaron, nobody will be interrupting or joining you this evening." Devlin folded her dress, picked up her stilettos, and turned to walk away.

"It was a pleasure to meet you, Mr. Simon. I am confident that you will have a great evening. I hope that we get to see more of you."

What the hell did that mean?

"Um, thank you, Mr. Smith. It was nice meeting you, also, sir."

Aaron was beyond uncomfortable at this point. The erection he had in the car had long subsided.

Fuck.

He just realized he didn't have a ride home. If he ran out of there now, how would he get home?

The First Lesson

Mrs. Smith could tell that he was nervous now. She and Devlin had enjoyed teasing him, but she did not want that to put a damper on the evening.

Still holding his hand, she guided Aaron into another room. The shower had been running for some time. Condensation covered the bathroom mirror. Steam enveloped the room as she opened the shower door.

"Come."

Slowly, he stripped off his clothes. This was much less of a performance than at the club. He was anxious.

I should not be doing this.

Abandoning his better judgment, Aaron still climbed into the shower.

Too late now.

Shyly, he stood in the corner. He cupped himself to hide his nakedness.

Mrs. Smith shook her head with disappointment. "I figured I would have to do this."

"Aaron, I do not have a lot of hangups. If there is something I want to do, a woman, an orgy, being airtight… I will do it."

33

What the hell is airtight?

I rarely even bother with a safe word.

Safe word? What is she talking about?

"But what I will NOT do is hair!

She paused, hoping that he would catch on. The bewilderment on his face made it clear that he did not.

"I loathe the taste of hair in my mouth. His, hers, or theirs. It does not matter to me. You said earlier you wanted to trust me. Time to gauge how sincere you were."

She kissed him, passionately and deeply. She grabbed the engorged tip of his penis and held it firmly. She looked at Aaron with mischievous eyes.

Aaron didn't notice where the straight razor had come from in her other hand. He flinched but did not move because of her tight grip.

"Are you ready, lover?"

"I am Mrs. Smith," he gulped, standing firm.

She knelt, never loosening her grip on Aaron's dick or the razor. With surgical precision, she shaved him from back to front. Starting from his underside, she never took her eyes off Aaron. Without having ever touched him before, Mrs. Smith knew every curve of his flesh.

Aaron would have marveled at her skills, except that he was terrified. Nonetheless, he relinquished all control. He wanted the reward, whatever it was.

"I am finished. I need you to always keep yourself just as I have done for you. Now rinse yourself off, please."

Aaron reached for the detachable shower nozzle and began to wash himself. Mrs. Smith never moved from her spot. The soap escaped down the drain. Painfully erect, his dick moved about as if it were looking for her.

It found her. Or, more accurately, she found it. Her lengthy tongue touched the head of his dick. She flicked it softly. In appreciation, it spasmed with each touch from her.

Please put it in your mouth. Please God…

The water had thoroughly drenched her majestic crown as she finally took Aaron in her mouth.

Fuuuccckkkk

It was indeed a reward worth working for and waiting for. Aaron was not a virgin, but he was not that experienced either. He had only been sucked twice before. He thought that it was great. They were nothing compared to this.

She isn't even using her hands.

There was a constant sensation through all her movements. He couldn't place it, but it just felt like something was running back and forth along the length of his shaft.

"Wha…what is that…. fuck…that feels…shit that feels so good."

She slid her mouth off his shaft. She looked him intensely in the eye. Smiled. Stuck her tongue out. It was pierced.

How did I miss that?

She took every inch of him in… to the base.

The shower head finally dropped from his hands. Water violently sprayed everywhere. The bathroom floor was soaked.

Mrs. Smith grabbed the flailing sprinkler and faced it upwards between Aaron's legs.

What the hell…

The water hit his anus and his balls at the same time. The water sprayed upward in a tight and heated stream. His legs weakened.

She would not let him cum, she continued to edge him, feeling his breathing become more erratic, his balls start to swell, his dick becoming more engorged.

He could not concentrate between the two sensations. He was overwhelmed. He felt the eruption developing.

Instinctively, he reached for her head.

The stinging smack of her skin against his wet ass brought him back to reality. She abruptly stopped, stood up, and got out of the shower.

"I…I…, I'm sorry… I mean, I apologize, Mrs. Smith. Did I do something wrong?"

Deviously, she smiled.

"Come here Aaron," she ordered while pointing to the floor mat beside her.

Compliantly, he stepped out and stood before her.

Follow My Instructions

They left the downstairs shower. Dutifully, he followed her. They climbed the winding, carpeted stairwell to her lavish bedroom, him trailing her. They passed countless doorways to get to their destination. At the end of a hallway stood a single door. The code was punched into the keypad. A gasp of air echoed softly as the door opened.

The bedroom was larger than his entire childhood home. The deep oak and auburn décor contrasted with the sterile eggshell color scheme of the rest of the house. It looked out of place in the house, but it felt like home. This refuge, being with her, was a need that he never knew he had.

The fireplace exploded into life from a switch behind the bedroom bar. Mrs. Smith poured Aaron another small drink.

The reflection of the flames danced in her eyes as she looked up at Aaron. Pulling him close from the nape of his neck, they kissed passionately. Her teeth tugged slightly on his bottom lip. He tasted a faint hint of iron and leaned deeper into the kiss.

Abruptly, she pulled away from him and walked to the bed. The now raging fireplace accented every curve of her goddess-like body.

"Come here, Aaron. Stand over me. Let me worship you."

He climbed onto the bed as if it were a sacred throne. He loosely held onto the crisscrossing bars of the wrought-iron four-poster bed. His legs were weak. The reinforced steel held him upright as his balance wavered. On her knees, Mrs. Smith picked up a circular object from her side.

"What is that?"

"This is what you call a cock ring. You will wear this, and it will keep your penis hard and full of cum for me. You will feel all the blood rush to that beautiful dick of yours—longer, for me to enjoy. That is what it is."

She put him back in her mouth. Blood was filling him again. It did not take long for him to return to his full self after being edged all day. He was throbbing. Before he became completely erect, she slid the cock ring on him.

Aaron instantly felt the restriction on his dick and on his balls. Veins bulged more deeply than he had ever noticed.

"I want you to feed me. I want you to stroke it until I tell you to stop."

He nodded compliantly. "Yes, Mrs. Smith."

"You will not cum until I allow you to. Do you understand?"

"Yes, Mrs. Smith."

"If you think you are going to cum, you need to stop. Only, and I mean only, once I have allowed it, you will give me all your hot cum. Do you understand, Aaron? Would you like that?"

"Yes ma'… yes, I would, Mrs. Smith. Very much."

Aaron's dick was beyond sensitive. His own first touch sent spasms through his body. He held tighter to the bars, hoping they did not give way.

The game of cat and mouse, pleasure and denial, went on for quite some time. She would lick him as he stroked himself. It did not matter the pace he wanted to touch himself; she dictated it. When he was close, neither of them touched him. He was forced to watch as she pleasured herself. Her own hands allowed her to cum repeatedly. When she was tired of her hands, she used a small wand-like toy to massage her clit and to slide inside of her.

Aaron, however, was not allowed any relief. Watching her, unable to do anything, was agonizing. Periodically, she removed the cock ring. Nonetheless, he was not relieved; she kept putting it back on him.

He learned a level of restraint that he never had reason to believe existed. It was brutal. He was lightheaded and weak.

Just as he felt he could not go on, she snatched the cock ring off him. Aaron abruptly exploded. He could not control it. All his semen fled the prison Mrs. Smith had created. Each spasm was more intense than the previous one. The pleasure was inexplicably intensified.

Enormous amounts dropped onto her waiting face. What missed her face landed on her breasts as if it could target her.

With one hand, he grappled the crossbars to maintain his balance. The sensation, regardless of the pleasure, was debilitating. The other hand feverishly stroked his dick until only droplets remained.

She relished bathing in his cum. She was ravenous, grabbing for it before it could even land on her. She rubbed it deeper into her face and breasts.

Aaron didn't want to touch himself anymore. It compounded the intensity further. He could not help it.

He succumbed to the euphoric feeling and fell onto the bed. Mrs. Smith did not seem even to notice him at that moment. She was playing with the cum.

He wanted to please her, so he began to help her. He smeared it onto her breasts. Her hands controlled his. They guided him on how to touch her. Soft and Hard. The pleasure of pain. She loved his initiative.

Next Lessons

She then told him it was time for him to learn. He pleasured her based on his own skill set. She was pleased with how much he knew. Nonetheless, she dominated him and instructed him on what she liked.

Her body spoke to him. They were inexplicably coordinated, moving in an intertwined rhythm. Sexual skills surfaced that had not existed for him before this moment. He was a different man. Possessed in this moment.

Once again, she grabbed Aaron's hand. She folded his thumb and pinkie finger inward, leaving three fingers extended.

"Curve your fingers upward for me. Do you feel that soft and textured spot on your fingers? It feels full, doesn't it? That spot is now your best friend."

Mouth still full, tasting her juices, he only nodded.

"Keep your mouth on me, licking and sucking my clit. You will do one more thing with those three fingers. I want you to gesture for me to come here."

"Do you understand?"

He did not. Aaron nodded negatively but never stopped sucking and licking.

"You will continue to curl your fingers back, as if you are gesturing for me to come here. Your fingers will keep pressing against that beautiful spongy spot that you feel at the top of my pussy."

He found her G-spot after fumbling around for a moment. But when he got it right, she let out a "fuuccckkk."

That was all the approval he needed. He kept gesturing, and she kept screaming and writhing around in pleasure. She had pulled out that same wand again, but it was too intense. She threw it across the room, knocking over a bottle or vase. They could not tell and did not slow down to figure it out.

It did not take Aaron long to get her to that moment, that moment when she would explode more intensely than any other time that evening.

"Don't stop, Daddy, make this pussy explode. Fuck that pussy, Daddy, please…"

Huh? Daddy. Me?

Aaron struggled to regain his focus on her instructions. Her words left him excited and confused.

"Please make me squirt, baby. Make this pussy cum all over you!"

Is she begging for me? Is she for real?

"Daddy, can I cum? Can I soak your face?" Oh shit, Daddy, it's cumming…"

Is she begging for me? Is she for real?

"Oh shit, can you feel it, Daddy? Can you feel it? Are you gonna make that pussy cum? Oh fuck, Daddy, don't swallow, please. I want it back... Fuck, I'm coming, I'm coming, I'm..."

She was no longer comprehensible. She let out a barrage of curse words, foreign languages, and struck him on the head and shoulders. She was completely out of control.

...Meanwhile, her pussy was squirting like the fountain from the club. Her geyser was spraying onto Aaron's face. He caught some in his mouth and his mustache. Most of it was dripping off him onto the now-soaked bed.

She regained some control. She pulled Aaron close to her and kissed him. She sealed his mouth with hers. Airtight. She inhaled all her juices from her mouth.

She thrust Aaron's drink to his face, gesturing for him to drink it. She pulled him back to her lips in another passionate kiss. Mixing the taste and texture of her ejaculation with the flavor of bourbon.

She swallowed it, tilting her head back so that it fully descended her throat. She relished the last few drops, licking the remnants from the sides of her mouth and, when she was done, from Aaron's mouth as well.

He caught himself staring in awe. This evening continues to be unlike anything he has ever experienced. Coming out of her own trance-like state, she realizes that Aaron is staring in bewilderment.

"You are indeed a fast study." Her tap on the bed beckoned him to lie down beside her.

She lifted her leg and mounted her stallion before placing the cock ring back on him. Aaron's erection had fully returned. The cock ring was full once again from his renewed girth. She straddled him. Slowly, she slid him inside her. With each movement, her walls gripped his shaft deeper and tighter. The pulsating veins massaged her walls.

"Do not look away. Look at me."

He willingly submitted, unable to look away. Her body was perfect. Angelic, flawlessly beautiful. Her hair had dried, and every hair had returned to its place.

Her pace quickened. Her thrusts became more aggressive. His penis struck the back of her vagina. He was in her stomach at this point. It hurt him in the most pleasurable of ways. He lost all concentration. All that was left was instinct.

He squeezed harder on her hips, subconsciously trying to slow her pace.

She grabbed both of his hands and leaned in more. She wrapped them around her throat. She controlled them again. Squeezing tighter. Airways constricted. Wheezing through each stroke.

When it was not hard enough, she slapped Aaron for the second time tonight. He did not mind it at all this time.

"Harder!"

His grip tightened. Nails now dug into her flesh. He adjusted his legs to brace himself. He matched take cadence of her aggressive bucking. Then, he surpassed it.

The intensity increased. It was not clear what sounds she had made. A shriek. A growl. Something Beastlike. She leaned deeply into him. Back deeply arched for the deepest stimulation. One hand massaged her clitoris violently. The other hand latched onto his shoulders. Bodies pulled closer. Nails pierced flesh. Blood stained the sheets. Flesh pounded decadently into flesh.

Their eyes struggled to match each other's glare. She knew he was cumming soon. So was she.

She sat back up. She wanted to feel him fully, deep inside.

"Cum inside of me, Aaron."

Once again, she had caught him off guard, but his stroke did not change.

"Can I? I mean…. You are married."

"Not what I said, Aaron! Would you like to cum inside of me?

"I want to feel all that you have left, deep inside of me. Give your cum to me. It is mine. I want it, Daddy."

"You will give me what I want, won't you, Daddy? You have been so good to me, Daddy. Aren't you proud of yourself? I am Daddy."

Fuck she is so beautiful. I shouldn't. Imma hold it. Imma…

He failed. She saw the look on his face. He was trying to think about it. Not an option for her. She gripped his dick tighter than she had before. She stole his cum from him.

Aaron let out a growl that echoed throughout the bedroom. The sensation was unprecedented. cumming inside of her was even better than when he came the first time that night. He had never felt like that before. Every nerve in his dick was on fire. He could not stop convulsing.

She was merciless. Ferociously, she fucked him throughout his orgasm. Cum ejaculated deep inside her. She could feel every warm drop.

Unwanted tears trickled from his eyes. She climbed down from her perch atop him. His dick was still convulsing. Glistening with their combined juices. She pounced on him as if he were prey. Ferally, she lapped up every remaining drop of him.

Once thoroughly drained, they both lay there. Spent. Sweating. Panting. Both of their bodies are now sore from the pleasure and punishment.

She lay there, eyes closed, silent, regaining her composure. She eventually adjusted her body to lean in and whisper in Aaron's ear.

"That was so needed. Hmmmm. You have been worth every dollar."

"You did so well in following directions, Aaron. I had a small fraction of uncertainty, but you made me a believer. We will be keeping you."

"We, Mrs. Smith?" Aaron felt his nervousness return.

"Please, call me Lydia." Her lips met his one last time that night, but it was far from their last kiss in the year to come.

Postgraduate

Graduation came in no time. His parents were so proud that not only was he the first person in the family to graduate, but he also did so with honors. Lydia gave him a Rolex Emperor when she celebrated with him that evening.

Rather than going straight to Graduate School, Aaron began working at a Fortune 500 company directly out of college. As part of his graduation gift, Mrs. Smith made a call on his behalf to a friend. The next thing he knew, he was reading his name on a driver's tablet at the baggage area at LaGuardia International Airport.

At 24, he was making over six figures at his company. However, his salary paled in comparison to the unmarked envelopes, wire transfers, allowance, and continuous gifts that he received from Mrs. Smith and her network.

Once she vouched for how professional, discreet, and talented he had become, his extracurricular calendar remained full. These were women and couples who also had more money than time. They clearly understood the value of Aaron's services.

And he was compensated handsomely.

Epilogue

Aaron was snatched away from his reminiscing by an intrusive watch alert. He thought he had muted it, but he was mistaken. At least it was good news. Mrs. Clay had deposited his fee into the account.

The sauna door slowly closed behind him. It was time to get on with the day. Returning to his condo, Aaron laid out his suit, shirt, and accessories before hopping in the shower.

Feeling refreshed, he sat down to his black cup of coffee and fruit before turning on the monitors in his kitchen. As he sipped on his coffee, he browsed through several news, market, and sports updates.

This was his routine. He enjoyed starting this part of the morning quietly and without disturbance. But not today.

For the third time this morning, he was disrupted by his phone. A straightforward text from Edwin read, "Let's talk please. Lucia needs to be tightened up AGAIN."

Chuckling to himself, "Mrs. Sullivan must be having another temper tantrum." He gave the message a "thumbs up" as he placed his empty coffee cup inside the dishwasher.

Author's Last Thoughts

Above all else—thank you.

Thank you for reading, for trusting me with your time, and for stepping into this world. I'm building one chapter at a time. I do not take that lightly. Whether this is your first book with me or you have been here since my earliest nonfiction projects, I appreciate you more than you know.

Next, please take the time to share your thoughts on this work (and any of my other works) with honest reviews on Amazon and/or Goodreads. Your opinions matter, and they help other readers like you find these works.

Amazon:
https://www.amazon.com/author/anthony.scott.esq.

Goodreads:
https://www.goodreads.com/author/show/56878579.Anthony_Scott

Now the critical part… What's next?

Aaron's story is just getting started. You will learn so much more about him and his ascent (or descent) into this world. More (not all) of his evolution, his temptations, and the doors he should have never opened will be revealed in *Meet the Sullivans: More Money than Time: Book 2.*

...and believe me, Mrs. Smith is nowhere near done with him. She just introduced him to a lifestyle that is intoxicating, powerful, and extremely hard to walk away from. Would you be able to walk away from it?

For those of you who felt something... unsettling... whenever the world of "The Vault" was mentioned, you were not imagining it.

Yes, Ursula said what she said!

You will absolutely learn more about her, about Misty, about the Twins, and about the many other beautifully dangerous souls who play in that world within this universe.

If your mind went back to certain scenes and you caught yourself thinking, *"Something about that wasn't normal..."* Good. Hold onto that (insert devilish wink here. lol).

Later in 2026, I hope that you will join me in *The Vault*, an erotic horror series set in a lifestyle club with no map, no rules, and no boundaries. Desires. Fantasies. Fetishes. Danger (and descent) all live within those "walls."

Finally, before you go, I'd love to stay connected with you.

If you want early access to future chapters, opportunities to be a Beta or ARC Reader, or updates on contests and giveaways, sign up for the newsletter by visiting <u>www.isipublishingllc.com</u>

This universe is only getting bigger, deeper, and wilder from here.

Thank you for taking the first steps into it with me.

— T. Scott

About the Author

T. Scott is the pen name used by Anthony W. Scott, Esq. for his erotic fiction, including the *More Money Than Time* multi-book series and the erotic-horror series *The Vault*, both launching in 2026. Under this name, he writes stories that explore power, desire, and the consequences that follow when boundaries are tested, ignored, and/or indulged in.

Writing as Anthony W. Scott, Esq., he is an attorney, public speaker, and the author of *Unlocking Potential: Insights, Tips & Strategies for Young Black Professionals* and *Overcoming Imposter Syndrome: You Belong at the Table*. Also in 2026, he will release another non-fiction work, *Fitting 25 into 24: Time, Energy & Boundary Management for High Achievers*. These works center on leadership, identity, and navigating high-pressure spaces with intention.

The distinction between these names is intentional. One examines discipline and growth. The other confronts temptation and control.

https://www.isipublishingllc.com

https://linktr.ee/Isipublishingllc.com

https://www.isipublishingllc.com/contact-1

Also by Anthony Scott

T. Scott writes provocative, character-driven fiction that explores power, desire, and the boundaries people cross when ambition and temptation collide.

Anthony W. Scott, Esq. writes non-fiction focused on leadership, professional growth, and navigating self-doubt, drawing from his experience as an attorney, public servant, and speaker.

Unlocking Potential: Insights, Tips & Strategies for Young Black Professionals.

"How can I be my authentic self at work? Can I wear braids? Should I cut my dreads or leave them tied back?"

"How can I find a mentor when I'm the only one who looks like me?"

"Why does it feel like I'm working twice as hard without recognition? Have I stayed too long?"

These are questions many African American professionals ponder while advancing in their careers. Unlocking Potential: Tips, Insights, and Strategies for Young Black Professionals helps the reader navigate their professional and personal lives. It is intended to serve as a guide to help younger professionals avoid the pitfalls of previous generations. It contains practical tips, quotes, and examples to enhance your career and show how these concepts apply in practice.

Overcoming Imposter Syndrome:
You Belong at the Table!

Have you ever felt like you're just faking it—like one day, everyone will realize you don't really belong in the room? Even after earning degrees, promotions, accolades, and respect, many high achievers carry a quiet, exhausting fear that they're not good enough. That fear has a name: Imposter Syndrome.

In Overcoming Imposter Syndrome: You Belong at the Table!, I take readers on a powerful journey through the minds and hearts of professionals from all walks of life who've battled this invisible burden. Through a blend of personal experience and candid interviews, this book reveals how imposter syndrome shows up across industries, identities, and backgrounds—and how to overcome it.

While this struggle uniquely shapes the experiences of women, people of color, and first-generation professionals, imposter syndrome is universal. From lawyers to creatives, educators to entrepreneurs, the stories within reflect a broad, diverse spectrum of voices—each offering insight, vulnerability, and strength.

This book isn't about perfection. It's about truth. It's about learning to silence the inner critic and finally embrace the fact that you do belong.

Whether you're just getting started or leading at the highest levels, this book is a reminder:

You didn't get here by accident.

You belong at the table.

Meet the Sullivans:
More Money than Time: Book 2

Coming Soon (E-Book only)

Meet the Sullivans continues the story of Aaron Simon. He is no longer naive or innocent—that man is gone.

Now, Aaron moves through the professional world polished, intelligent, articulate, and respected. Disciplined in his work and deliberate in his presence, he commands attention without demanding it.

Beyond that world, Aaron is also a highly sought-after escort—selective, discreet, and impeccably professional. His appeal isn't merely physical; it's the way he listens, leads, and creates a connection that lingers.

Lucia and Edwin Sullivan believe they're indulging a fantasy they can manage—something purely sexual, contained, and transactional. What they don't yet know is whether Aaron will quietly unsettle the balance of their marriage—or become precisely what it's been missing.

This isn't just sex. It's intimacy, permission, and the vulnerability that comes with wanting more.

Meet the Sullivans is where desire tests boundaries—and connections take shape.

The Vault: Book I

Coming Soon (E-Book only)

The Vault is not a place you stumble into.

It is a private, invitation-only lifestyle club where anything goes— as long as the ever-present hostess, Ursula, allows it.

Within its walls, The Vault offers something for everyone: pleasure and passion, indulgence and fetish, power and surrender.

But it is not built on desire alone. It also houses vengeance, retribution, and agony.

What you witnessed in *Yes, Mrs. Smith* was only a glimpse of The Vault's prestige, its allure, its decadence.

The Vault exists everywhere and nowhere at once. It is a whispered name. A sealed door.

If you've been invited behind its walls, understand this, it was not accidental.

What awaits you may become your most intoxicating fantasy… or the beginning of your undoing. Either way, you will not leave untouched.

You do not find The Vault. It finds you, your secret fantasies, your hidden sins, and the parts of yourself you thought were buried forever.

Fitting 25 into 24: Time, Energy & Boundary Management for High Achievers.

Coming in 2026.

Fitting 25 Hours into 24: Time, Boundaries, and Energy Management for High Achievers is for those who are tired of feeling overwhelmed and constantly behind. What if the problem isn't needing more time but using the time you have more effectively?

This book challenges the hustle mindset by introducing the 25-Hour Framework—a system designed to help you focus on high-impact work, set boundaries that stick, and reclaim control of your schedule.

Have you ever finished a long day only to feel like you accomplished nothing meaningful? Inside, you'll learn how to eliminate busywork, master the art of saying no without guilt using the Polite No Formula, and align your tasks with what truly matters through the Passion Pyramid.

Whether you're an early-career professional trying to avoid burnout, a mid-career leader drowning in meetings, or an entrepreneur struggling to balance work and life, this book offers a blueprint for working smarter—not harder.

If you're ready to stop feeling overwhelmed and start managing your time with purpose, Fitting 25 Hours into 24 is your guide.

www.ingramcontent.com/pod-product-compliance
Lightning Source LLC
Chambersburg PA
CBHW071505130726
47997CB00006B/2449